Chapter 1

Jack was running out of school.

The bell hadn't gone and the rest of the school were still hard at work. But Jack was off and running. No one ran after him. No one ever did. No one could catch him.

Running out of school was the one thing he was good at. He should be, he did it every week. Jack was 14 years old, and fast.

Sometimes he ran because a new teacher asked him to read out loud in class. Sometimes he panicked when the work got too hard for him. Sometimes the other kids made fun of his spelling. Sometimes the school day just got too long for him.

Today he had said something in class that made everyone fall about laughing.

He'd been in history with Mrs Jenkins. He liked her and he felt safe with her. She always went over things with him and gave him worksheets he could read. She had just helped him plan out his work.

"Good. Get started and I'll come back later," she said.

"Thanks, Mum," he said.

The word, 'Mum', was out of his mouth before he could stop it. The rest of the class fell about laughing.

"Jack's got his mum with him," said Bill.

"Are you taking him home with you tonight, Mrs Jenkins?" asked Ellie.

Jack went red in the face, and anger began rising up inside him. He was on his feet in a flash. Over went his chair and his work fell to the floor.

He was off!

The class gave a cheer as he went dashing out of the room. He was angry. He was upset, and he couldn't stop running.

He raced past classrooms, banging on doors. He dashed downstairs, four steps at a time. He ran through the cloakroom, pulling coats off pegs. No one was going to stop him.

Jack jumped up three steps and went skidding round a corner. Suddenly, he had to sidestep Mr Benson as he came out of the staff room.

"Bye, Jack. See you tomorrow," said Mr Benson.

Jack ripped some artwork off the wall and kept going. As he ran to the main doors, someone else shouted, "Bye, Jack. See you tomorrow." It was Mr Johnson, the Head. He'd seen Jack run out of school more times than he'd had a school dinner. He knew he'd be back.

"I'm never coming back to this school again!" shouted Jack, as he burst through the doors.

He hated the school, he hated the teachers and he hated the kids. He turned round as he got to the school gates.

"I'll burn this school down one day. You see if I don't!" he shouted. Then he ran off up the road.

That night, part of the school burnt to the ground.

Chapter 2

It was the knocking on the door that woke Jack up the next morning. Then, the banging on the door that made him get out of bed and go downstairs. The flap of the letter-box was open and someone was looking at him as he walked to the door.

"Open the door please, Jack. We want a word with you," said someone.

Jack's mum and dad were on holiday and his older sister was at work. He didn't open the door.

"This is the police, Jack. Now be a good lad and open the door."

Jack opened the door, and looked up at two of the biggest policemen he had ever seen. It was 10 a.m. and this was a bad start to the day. The rest of his day was about to go downhill, fast.

The policemen asked him where his parents were, and then where his sister worked. They asked him to get dressed and get into the police car. At the police station, he sat in a small room with the two policemen.

"We've sent for your sister," said the big policeman on his right.

"Do you mind having a chat while we wait?" asked the even bigger policeman on his left.

"No," said Jack. "But what's it about?"

"When did you do it, Jack?" asked the big policeman.

"Do what? I don't know what you're on about," said Jack.

"When did you set fire to your school?" asked the even bigger policeman.

"I didn't set fire to my school," said Jack.

"Did you shout the words, 'I'll burn this school down one day. You see if I don't?'" asked the big one.

Jack didn't speak.

"Well, did you shout those words when you ran out of school yesterday?" asked the bigger one.

"Yes," said Jack.

"So when did you set fire to the school?" asked the big one.

"I didn't set fire to the school," said Jack.

"Is it the flames you like, or the fire engines racing down the road?" asked the bigger one.

9

Jack didn't speak.

"Or do you hate school so much you just wanted to burn it down?" the big one asked.

"I don't hate school. I like school," said Jack.

"You like school? How can you like school when you spend so much time running away from it?" asked the bigger one.

"I like it some of the time," said Jack.

The two policemen just looked at each other. Then they looked at Jack.

"I hope you're not trying to be funny, Jack," said the big one.

Jack began to feel unwell. "Can I go to the toilet, please?" he asked.

"Not yet," the two policemen said at the same time.

"Come on Jack, just tell us how you did it. You'll feel better when you've told us," said the bigger one, who seemed as wide as he was tall.

"But I didn't do it," said Jack.

"We think the fire was started at midnight. So where were you at that time?" asked the big one.

"I was asleep in bed. You can ask my sister. She's looking after me this week," said Jack.

"We'll ask your sister as soon as she gets here. We've sent a car for her," said the bigger one, who seemed too big for the room.

Jack began to get a pain in his belly.

"Do you sleep in the same room as your sister?" asked the big one.

"No," said Jack.

"So you could have crept out of the house when your sister went to bed. You could have walked the mile to school and set fire to it. Then you could have crept back into the house again," said the bigger one, who seemed as big as Shrek.

"But I didn't," said Jack. "Can I go to the toilet now, please? I need to go badly."

The big one said, "And we badly need to know why, how and when you set fire to the school."

Then the bigger one said, "You see, Jack. We think you did it. You've been running out of school and shouting about burning it down for a long time. And now you've done it. You're in a lot of trouble, young man."

Jack was now feeling frightened, and he had cramps in his belly.

His fear began oozing out of him. The smell was so bad that the two policemen stepped back.

"Oh, no," gasped the big one.

"Oh, hell!" shouted the bigger one.

"I told you I needed the toilet," said Jack.

The two policemen got out of the room as fast as they could.

Then one of them shouted, "Get him out of that room and get him cleaned up."

Someone came in and took Jack to the toilets and left him there. Jack looked at himself in the mirror. He didn't look good, he didn't feel good, and he didn't smell good.

He could do something about the smell but he would still be in a mess. He would still be trapped inside a police station. And Jack didn't like feeling trapped.

He looked around as he sorted himself out and dumped his underpants in the bin.

He was in an old toilet with old windows. They were windows that a 14-year-old boy, who was small for his age, could get out of. So he did.

Then he ran off down the road muttering, "I'll burn your police station down, one day. You see if I don't."

Chapter 3

Jack had never been top of his class.
He had never been first at anything.
But he was now. He was the first from his
school to run away from a police station.

That was Jack's problem. He was better
at running than he was at thinking. He did
have a brain. He wasn't the cleverest thing
on two legs, but he did have a brain.

He just forgot to use it sometimes.
He wasn't using it now.

Running away from a problem is silly.
Running away from school is very silly.
But running away from a police station is
just stupid.

Jack was starting to work this out
for himself as he ran down the road.
He looked back to see if a fleet of police
cars were coming after him. Or if police
dogs were being let off their leads so they
could catch him and pin him to the ground.
But, as far as he could see, there wasn't
even one policeman on a bike.

They would come after him. He knew
that. When they found him they would
not be happy. They wouldn't like being
out-smarted by a 14-year-old boy.

Jack stopped running and tried to think.
He needed to hide and make plans. Where
could he hide in the middle of town?

And how long did he have before the two biggest policemen on the planet came after him?

Jack looked in the window of a bookshop. He didn't want to get trapped inside a shop but standing around on the street wasn't too clever. He went in and made it look as if he was reading some of the books.

They were far too hard for him but he put on a good act. It was the same act he used at school. Going from shelf to shelf gave him time to rest and think. What could he do? Where could he go?

He couldn't go home, the police would go there. He couldn't go to his sister's work as she was on her way to the police station.

He couldn't get help from his mum and dad as they were on holiday in Greece. They wouldn't be home until the weekend.

He had to keep away from the police until his mum and dad came back. They would help him sort out this mess.

Jack went to the next shelf and picked up a book. The picture on the cover made him smile. The book was called, *My Life As A Clown*. His smile got bigger.

"It must be about me," he said to himself.

He opened the book. He couldn't read all the words but he could read the pictures. They showed a clown putting on his make-up. On went some cream, a red painted mouth, a wig and a funny nose. Suddenly, the man looked like someone else.

Jack stood looking at the book and thinking to himself. Maybe this was how he could hide. Not by making himself into a clown, but by changing the way he looked.

He put the book back on the shelf.
Then he went to the door of the shop
and looked up and down the street.

There were no policemen or police cars.
So he stepped out of the bookshop and
made his way to the joke shop.

Jack loved joke shops. He liked
everything about them: the tricks, the
masks, the stink bombs, the dog-turds
and the spiders.

He loved playing jokes on people.
The more he made people laugh, the more
friends he seemed to have.

The bell rang as he opened the door and
went inside. The shopkeeper looked up
and nodded to him. Jack nodded back and
started looking for the things he needed.
He tried on the wigs, the hats, the glasses,
the noses and the eye patch.

Jack made up his mind as he stood
looking at himself in the mirror.

He would just look very silly with all this stuff on, and it wouldn't fool anyone. The police would soon stop him if he went around dressed like this.

He put the things back and went to the door.

Then he froze as he saw two policemen go into the card shop on the other side of the street. What should he do? His head said, "stay", but his legs said, "go".

He listened to his legs and ran off down the road like a sprinter out of his blocks. It wasn't until he got into the next street that he stopped. He was panting like a dog and feeling frightened.

"I must be mad getting myself into this mess. Mad, mad, mad," he said to himself.

It was then that he knew what he was going to do.

Chapter 4

Jack kept a lookout for the police as he made his way out of town. He had a three-mile walk. He was heading for a small barn that was by the side of Moss End Wood.

That's where he would find Mad Mike. Mad Mike was a head case. He had to be. He had two bits of metal stuck in his brain.

He had been in the S.A.S. and a landmine had exploded, hitting him in the arms, legs and head. The doctors had said it was too risky trying to get the bits of metal out of his brain. They would have to stay there for the rest of his life.

He was lucky to be alive. But having the metal in his brain sometimes made him say, and do, odd things.

He had left the army and come to live just outside a village. Starting a new life hadn't been easy for him. It wasn't long before some people said he was a 'nutter' and began calling him Mad Mike.

Mad Mike agreed with them. He often shouted, "I used to be in the army, but now I'm barmy!."

Kids would sometimes shout at him and then run away. But Mad Mike never got angry.

He just kept working hard at patching up an old stone barn that a farmer sold him. And bit by bit, he made it into his new home.

Jack could see the barn as he jogged along the path by the side of Moss End Wood. As he got closer he slowed down to a walk. Going to see Mad Mike had seemed a good idea. But what was he going to say to him?

Jack stopped by a stone wall. He jammed his foot into the wall and pulled himself up. Now he could see the garden where Mad Mike grew some of his food.

And there he was! Walking up and down the garden pointing to his plants and talking to them. He was in full army battle dress. His boots were black, and clean, and shiny. His cap was pulled down over the left side of his head.

He had webbing round his waist with a dagger, bullets and a water bottle hanging from it. A hand gun was strapped to his hip.

"He is a nutter," Jack said to himself. "He's round the bend."

Jack dropped back down behind the wall and got closer to the gate. Now he could hear what Mad Mike was saying to his plants.

"Now come on, you lot. I want to see you doing better than this. You've got a lot more growing to do yet," he was saying.

Jack risked having a quick look over the gate. Mad Mike was striding along the path and stopping to speak to each patch of his garden.

"Now then, you peas, I can't see one pod, yet. What do you think you're doing?" he said. He strode over to the next patch.

"And you lot. Call yourself runner beans?
You haven't started walking yet. Get on
with it." He marched on up the garden.

"You spuds and carrots. How much
growing have you done, today?" Mad Mike
turned round and began striding back.
Then he yelled out, "I'll be back, same time
tomorrow. So get yourselves sorted out!"

Jack was trying hard not to laugh out loud.

Mad Mike helped him by shouting,
"And you, behind the wall. Stand up slowly
and put your hands in the air."

Jack's laughter died in his throat.
He stood up and looked over the gate.
Then his guts turned to water.

Mad Mike had his hand on the gun that
was on his hip.

"If you've come for my food, you'll have
to fight me for it," he said.

Jack couldn't speak. He was shaking
all over.

"Well? Are you friend or foe?" asked Mad Mike.

"Friend," said Jack, weakly.

"Then open the gate and walk slowly into the garden."

Jack did as he was told.

"Come a bit closer."

Jack went a bit closer. He could now smell the polish on Mad Mike's boots. He could see the medals on his chest. He could feel the pride this man had. Jack was shaking as he looked up at his face. Mad Mike seemed to be in a dream.

Jack said to him, "You know me. My name's Jack. I've been here before." Mad Mike looked at him. Then the dream seemed to pass and he slowly nodded his head.

"Yes. You're a friend. You can call me Mike. But you shouldn't creep up on a man like that. You could get yourself shot," he said.

Jack's eyes went back to the gun.
He could feel the sweat running down
his back. Mike watched him.

"It's never the gun that's the problem,
Jack. It's the man holding it. It's loaded but
the safety catch is on," he said.

Jack felt as if he was going to faint.
Mad Mike began walking to his barn.

"Come on, Jack. I'll make you a cup of
tea. You look as if you need one," he said.

They walked into the barn and Jack told
Mike all about the mess he was in.

Chapter 5

"Did you do it?" asked Mike.

"No," said Jack shaking his head.

Mike put his mug of tea down and pulled his chair closer to Jack.

"Look me in the eye," he said.

Jack looked into the eyes of a man who had seen war, and felt the blast of a landmine.

"Did you set fire to your school?"

Jack couldn't have lied if he tried.

"No, I didn't," he said.

After what seemed ages, Mike smiled and nodded his head. "So why did you keep shouting you'd burn the school down one day?" he asked.

"I get angry, sometimes. Then I run away from school and say I'll burn it down," said Jack.

"What makes you keep running away?" asked Mike.

"I don't know," said Jack. He could feel Mike's eyes looking right into his brain.

"I'll ask you again. What makes you so angry you have to run away from school?" he said.

Jack felt trapped. He couldn't lie to this man. He knew he wouldn't get away with it.

"I run away because I'm no good. I can't read. I can't spell. I can't keep up in lessons.

I can't do my homework. I can't even kick a football. I'm useless," he said.

He was close to tears.

"Is there anything you can do?" asked Mike.

"Yes. I'm good at running," said Jack.

"That should come in handy when the police come looking for you," smiled Mike. Jack didn't think it was funny. Mike sat back in his chair. "So why have you come to me?" he asked.

"I'm on the run from the police," Jack said. "But I don't know how to look after myself. You were trained by the S.A.S. You know all about it. So I've come to pick your brains."

As soon as he said the words, Jack wished he could take them back again.

"I wouldn't pick my brains, Jack. You'd get bits of metal in your fingers," said Mike.

Jack went red in the face. "I'm sorry. I didn't mean to make a joke about your brain," he said.

"That's all right. I've got used to it now," smiled Mike.

"Will you show me how to stay one step ahead of the police until my mum and dad get back?" asked Jack.

Mike shook his head. "You can't live your life like that. You might stay free for a day or two, but the police will track you down," he said.

Jack sat just sat there. He had hoped to get some help.

Mike said, "Look, Jack. You've spent your life running away from things. The only way you're going to get out of this mess is to find out who set fire to your school. Then you can take the proof to the police. I'll help you clear your name, but I won't help you go on the run."

Jack began getting the same feelings he got in school just before he did a runner. His hands were wet with sweat. His heart was beating faster and he could feel the panic rise up in him.

He got to his feet and shouted, "I can't clear my name. I don't know who set fire to the school. I just know it wasn't me. And if you won't help me, all I can do is keep running!" He turned, to run out of the barn.

Mike got to his feet and said, "You came here to ask me about my S.A.S. training. Well, that training isn't just about making shelters and finding food. It's also about how you act when you're in a mess."

He went on, "The S.A.S showed me that the real test of a man is what he does when everything seems to be against him. You're in that place right now, Jack. So what are you going to do?

"Run like a boy, or stand and fight like a man?"

Jack didn't know what to say.

"If you want to run, I won't help you. If you want to sort things out, I will," said Mike.

Jack shouted, "But I can't find out who set fire to the school. I haven't got the brains to do that. I can't think things out. All I can do is clown around!" Then he sat down, put his head in his hands, and cried.

Mike sat down beside him and said, "The reason you're finding it hard to stand up for yourself is because you don't like yourself very much. You see yourself as someone who fails at everything."

"Well, it's no fun being stupid," said Jack.

"Who said anything about being stupid?" said Mike.

"If you don't do well at school, you're stupid," said Jack.

Mike said, "That's not true. I wasn't good at school. I messed about and didn't listen. But I joined the army, worked hard, and sorted myself out."

Then he added, "I'd just got better at using my brain when I got in the way of a landmine."

He looked at Jack and said, "It's no good being angry at life, Jack. You've only got one. So get on and make the best of it."

Words like these had been said to Jack many times before but this time he listened to them.

"Right," said Mike, "let's see if we can get you out of this mess. We'll need to do what the S.A.S trained me to do. Think it. Plan it. Do it. Are you willing to have a go, Jack?" Jack nodded his head.

Mike said, "I'm going to need your brain for this. Don't forget, mine has got bits of metal in it."

Jack was feeling better about things now. "You mean, your brain has got bits of mine in it," he said.

Mike looked across at him. Then he put his head back and laughed out loud at the joke.

"That's better, Jack. Keep seeing the funny side of life. You'll have a much better time," he said.

Now it was time for two brains to start thinking about one plan.

Chapter 6

"So how do we start?" asked Jack.

"You start by making a list of the kids you know who might want to set fire to a school.

They may still be at school or have left. They may never have been to your school at all. They may have been expelled. Now start thinking," said Mike.

After a long time, Jack said, "I've got three names but my spelling isn't good."

"I'll help you," said Mike. The three names were put down on paper.

"Now, who is your best friend? Who would you trust with your life?" asked Mike.

Jack said, "No one. I don't have a best friend. I hang around with lots of kids because they know I'll give them a laugh. They know they can get me to be stupid. But I don't have a friend I trust."

Mike had stopped listening to him. His hands were on the back of his head, and his eyes were glazed over. Suddenly, he said, "We've got to get through the minefield. I'm going first. Leave a gap before you come after me."

Then he was down on his belly and inching his way across the floor. Sweat was trickling down his forehead as he moved.

Jack went cold with fear. Mike was having a flashback! What would happen to him if the mine went off?

He went over and sat down next to him. Mike pushed him away.

"Landmines. Get back, get back!" he shouted.

Jack grabbed hold of one of Mike's big hands. "It's OK, Mike. It's me, Jack. You're at home in your barn. All the landmines have gone."

Mike slowly looked at Jack. Then his glazed eyes began to clear.

"What the hell am I doing on the floor? Come on, Jack. We've got work to do," he said. The two of them sat down at the table.

"So, who did you say you'd trust with your life?" asked Mike. He was asking the same question he'd asked just before he'd dived onto the floor.

"I don't have someone I trust," said Jack.

Mike said, "You need a friend in your school who can go around asking questions. Someone will know something about this fire. And we need to check on the three names you put down. Is there no one you can trust?"

Jack was just about to shake his head when Anna came into his mind.

Anna was in the same year as him. She had wanted to go out with him, but he had been too shy to say yes. Maybe she would help him.

"There's a girl called Anna. She might help. But how can I talk to her?" asked Jack.

"Does she have a phone?" asked Mike.

"I've seen her on a mobile, but I haven't got her number," said Jack.

"Maybe she's on the phone at home. What's her surname and where does she live?" asked Mike.

"It's Heaton. And she lives in Brook Street," said Jack.

Mike reached over and took a phone book off the shelf. He found the number and wrote it on a pad.

"I didn't think you had a phone," said Jack.

"I haven't. It costs too much money to get a line out to this barn. And I hate bells and ring tones. The noise does my head in. I like to be left alone," said Mike.

"So what do we do next?" asked Jack.

"There's a phone box about a mile from here. We'll wait until it's dark to walk up there. Then you can phone Anna. If she can find anything out, she can leave you a note in a dead letter-box," said Mike.

"What's a dead letter-box?" asked Jack.

"It's somewhere she can leave a letter and we can pick it up. It can be a hole in a tree, under a stone, in a church," said Mike.

"We just have to think of a place and tell her."

"What if she won't help me? What if she goes to the police?" asked Jack.

"She won't know where you're phoning from. So you're safe," said Mike.

"And where can I hide away?" asked Jack.

"You can stay here for now. I'll put a camp bed in my workroom for you. I'll help you until your mum and dad get back," said Mike.

"But if the police find me here, you'll be in trouble too," said Jack.

"I'll take that risk. Life was getting dull around here. I still miss the army. I could do with a bit of fun," said Mike.

Jack didn't know what to think.

"Well? Are you game for this or do you want to give up?" asked Mike.

"I want to keep going," said Jack.

"Good man. Now let's get you some food," said Mike.

It was dark by the time they finished eating. Mike said, "Time for that phone call. It's about a mile to the phone box and I'm not going to use a torch. So stay close to me as we go."

Staying close to Mike wasn't easy. It was as if he could see in the dark. Jack had to jog some of the way just to keep up.

The path led them to a road. The phone box was about 50 metres up the road, just where the street lights started.

"I'll go first. You come and join me when I wave," said Mike.

Jack waited and then joined him in the phone box.

"Don't spend long making the call. And don't say who you are unless you are talking to Anna," said Mike.

Luck was on Jack's side.

As soon as he heard Anna's voice, he could see her long, brown hair and cheeky smile. He wished he'd said yes when he'd had the chance.

She told him she would find out what she could and leave him a letter just inside the door of St. John's church. She spoke very softly so no one in her house could hear.

As Jack put the phone down, Mike said, "Right. One more call. Ring your sister, tell her you're safe, and put the phone down."

Jack did as he was told. Then they were out of the phone box and back into the darkness of the night.

When they got back to the barn, Jack crashed out. He'd had a long day.

Chapter 7

It was daylight when Jack opened his eyes. The birds were in full song and the sun was shining into his bedroom. He got dressed and went to the open door of the barn. Mike was coming in with fresh eggs.

He looked at Jack and said, "About time, too. You could sleep for England."

He fried some eggs and made some toast. Soon Jack was sipping a cup of tea.

Mike said, "You can help me with some of my jobs, today. But it's best if you stay close to the barn, just in case someone comes round."

So Jack helped by feeding the chickens, chopping wood, planting seeds and mending part of a fence.

Mike didn't have any more flashbacks but he was still in full battle dress. He still walked and talked as if he was in the army.

"Come on, you chickens," he said in a loud voice. "I want more eggs than that. So come on, get laying."

When they were mending the fence he said, "We want a good job done here, Jack. We need a good strong fence. We don't want the enemy getting over this in the middle of the night."

Jack couldn't think who the enemy might be but he did as he was told.

Then it was time for Mike to go and see if Anna had left a letter in the church.

"Stay inside camp and don't open the door until I come back," he said to Jack.

He put on a coat and was off down the path. Jack went into the barn and waited.

When Mike came back, he had a letter in his hand and a smile on his face. Jack opened the letter and Mike helped him read it . . .

Dear Jack,

The police have been to school looking for you. We've been told to tell them, or a teacher, if we know where you are.

I've asked around but no one seems to know who set fire to the school. A lot of kids think you did it. BUT I DON'T. Look after yourself, wherever you are. Don't do anything silly.

Love Anna.

P.S. I'll write again if I hear anything.

P.P.S. The B.Bs are meeting tonight at The Fox and Hounds. It's all I know, sorry.

Jack dropped the letter onto the table and flopped down into a chair. "That's it then. The letter hasn't helped us. The school thinks I did it and the police are still after me. I might as well give up now," said Jack.

Mike wasn't listening to him. He'd picked up the letter and was reading it again.

"Who are The B.Bs?" he asked.

Jack said, "Just some stuck-up Sixth Formers who don't want to wear the school blazer. They want to choose what jackets they wear in school. But our school won't let them. So they started a club called The Blazer Boys. They meet in pubs now and then. They always put on posh-looking jackets for the meetings. I think they're sad."

"And they're meeting in The Fox and Hounds tonight," said Mike.

"So what?" asked Jack.

"I think I'll go down to the pub and have a look at them," said Mike.

"How's that going to help us? Even if they do know something, they're not going to tell you, are they?" said Jack.

"You mean they're not going to talk to me because I'm Mad Mike the crazy army man?"

Jack wished he'd kept his mouth shut.

"They won't have to talk to me," Mike said. "I'll just listen to them. It's a funny thing, but when people think you're not right in the head, they also think you haven't got ears. They keep on talking as if you're not there. I'll just sit in the pub with my newspaper and listen."

"You'll be lucky if you can hear yourself think in that pub. They play really loud music," said Jack.

After a meal Mike went to the pub.

Jack did the washing up and waited for him to return.

It was a long wait. By 10 p.m. Jack was in bed. He was tired, fed up, and thinking of giving up.

By 11 p.m. Mike was leaving the pub. He had his newspaper under his arm and a smile on his face.

Chapter 8

Jack woke up to the smell of breakfast being cooked. He was up, dressed and in the kitchen in no time. The washing bit could come later.

The frying pan was sizzling and spitting with eggs, bacon, sausages and black pudding. It was a sound and smell that Jack loved.

"Come and get this down you. It's going to be a long day," said Mike.

"I was thinking of going to the police today," said Jack.

"So was I. Just as soon as we've got the proof that The Blazer Boys set fire to your school," said Mike.

Jack's mouth fell open.

"With a mouth that size I think I'll need a bigger frying pan," smiled Mike.

"What did you say?" asked Jack.

"You sit and fill your belly and I'll tell you about last night," said Mike.

He went on, "The thing about loud pubs is that people shout a lot. And your Sixth Form friends did a lot of shouting."

"They're not my friends," said Jack, as he pushed the black pudding to the side of his plate.

Mike said, "I could only hear bits of what they were saying.

"But I think the bits add up."

"Add up to what?" asked Jack, getting egg all over his chin.

"One of them said, 'Meet at the old hall on Thursday. Lighting up time is 9 p.m. He's got something new. It's a cracker'," said Mike.

Jack said, "Is that all? But that doesn't mean they set fire to the school."

"Think about the words they were using. 'Lighting up'. 'Cracker'," Mike said.

"It still doesn't tell us much," said Jack.

"Think about the name they've called themselves," said Mike.

"The Blazer Boys. So what?" asked Jack.

"Don't just think about school blazers, Jack. I think the name means more than just jackets," said Mike

Jack still looked puzzled.

"What's another name for fire?" asked Mike.

The penny dropped. "A blaze!" said Jack.

"That's right. So a 'Blazer Boy' could be someone who starts a fire," said Mike.

"But we haven't got proof," said Jack.

"No, we haven't. But we've got a name, a time and a place," said Mike.

"So what do we do?" asked Jack.

"We have to be at that meeting. We have to see what The Blazer Boys are up to," said Mike.

"But we don't know where the old hall is," said Jack.

"I think I do. There's a big old house about a mile out of town. No one has lived there for years. Its called New Hall," said Mike.

"But is today the Thursday they're talking about?" asked Jack.

"I don't know. All we can do is hope," said Mike.

Jack mopped up the rest of his food.

"So do we go to the police?" he asked.

"No," said Mike. "This is a job for the S.A.S." Then Mike winked at Jack and said, "I mean it's a job for J.A.M."

"What do you mean, J.AM.?" asked Jack.

"Jack. And. Mike," said Mike.

Jack smiled. Then he looked at Mike and hoped his brain would keep on working OK.

"So what does J.A.M. do now?" asked Jack.

"Like I said before, we think it, plan it, do it," said Mike.

By the afternoon, they had a plan. They would set off for New Hall as soon as it was dark and be there for 8 p.m. That would give them an hour to get into the house and find a place to hide.

"Always try to be one step ahead of your enemy," said Mike.

They would take torches and a crow bar.

"I'll give you a torch when we get there. We'll walk in darkness," said Mike.

He looked at a map and plotted the best way to go.

As soon as darkness fell, they set off for New Hall. An hour later they were there. It was hard keeping up with Mike in the dark. Jack fell a few times and was scratched and bleeding.

"Stay here. I'll look for a way in," said Mike.

As Jack waited, he watched clouds drift across the moon. He heard noises in the long grass, and felt the night air getting colder.

He jumped as a voice in the dark said, "It's no good. All the doors and windows have been boarded up. No one has been in there for a very long time."

Jack swore to himself. Then he asked, "Is there another big house around here?"

"No. But there's a small cottage next to this house. Come on. Stay close to me," said Mike.

It wasn't far to the cottage. Mike went all the way round it and found a way in.

One of the boards over a window was loose. He used the crow bar to get it off. The window pushed up easily.

"Stay here. I'm going inside to have a look," said Mike.

Jack waited again. This time he didn't jump when a voice in the darkness said, "Come on in. I think we're in luck."

Chapter 9

The cottage was old, cold and smelt stale.

"I'll check we haven't left footprints.
Then I'll put the board back, pull down the
window and draw the curtains," said Mike.

It was now pitch black in the cottage.

"Time for torches," said Mike. He handed
one to Jack. The two beams of light
showed a room with full-length curtains,

a carpet, two armchairs and a coffee table with a glass top. There was a door leading into a kitchen and some stairs went up to a small landing. The beam from Mike's torch went from the coffee table to the fireplace and back again.

"Do you see what I see?" he asked.

"What?" asked Jack.

"Fag ends in the fireplace and plastic cups under the coffee table." Mike picked up the cups and put them to his nose. "Someone was here not long ago. And they weren't drinking tea," he said.

"So we might be in the right place," said Jack.

"Maybe," said Mike.

They looked in the kitchen and tried the taps and the switch. But there was no water or light.

"We need a hiding place. Let's look upstairs," said Mike.

Each stair creaked as they went up. Then the wooden landing creaked as they went to look at the two bedrooms. Mike chose the second bedroom as the hiding place.

"If we leave the door open we should be able to hear what they're saying," he said.

"If they come," said Jack.

"If they come," nodded Mike. The two of them sat on the floor and waited.

"What happens if they come upstairs?" asked Jack.

"They'll get a shock," said Mike.

"But there are only two of us. There could be five or six of them," said Jack.

"Three of us," said Mike and he patted the gun that was strapped to his hip.

"Is it loaded?" asked Jack.

"That's for me to know and them to find out," said Mike.

Jack stopped asking questions.

"Are you frightened, Jack?" asked Mike.

"Yes," said Jack.

"That's OK. Even the brave get frightened. They just don't show it," said Mike.

Then the torches were turned off and the talking stopped. In the dark, Jack's heart beat faster and his hands were wet with sweat. They were the feelings he got just before he did a runner. But this time he stayed where he was.

At last Mike said, "I think they're here."

He was right. A window was being pushed up, and into the cottage stepped The Blazer Boys.

"Come on. Get that light on," said a voice.

"Not yet. You know the rules. No lights until the board is put back, the window shut, and the curtains closed," said another voice.

When a big flashlight was at last turned on, everyone cheered.

"Right, I'll get the bottle open. You pass the fags round," said a voice. When this had been sorted out, someone asked, "Has everyone got a drink?"

"Yes!" they all shouted.

"OK. First of all let's drink to a job well done."

There were more cheers. Then voices said, "No one saw us go in or come out."

"But everyone saw the flames."

"And the fire engines."

"And the police."

"And the police put the blame on poor old Jack."

Everyone cheered again. Then someone said, "So let's drink to poor old Jack."

The cups were filled again.

"To Jack."

"What a prat."

"Thick as a brick."

"All he can do is run."

"All he can do is shout, 'I'll burn the school down one day'."

"But he didn't. We did. And he's got the police looking for him now."

Upstairs, Jack started to get to his feet. Mike put a hand on his arm to stop him. Then he put his mouth close to Jack's ear and said, "Don't get angry. Get even. Put names to the voices."

Downstairs, someone said, "Wow, this is strong stuff. Where did you get it from, Fishy?"

"From home. It's my dad's. He won't miss it. He's got loads."

"Fishy Fisher," Jack said to himself.

"All right you Blazers. I've got something new to show you," said a voice. There were more cheers and more drinks.

"Now, when we set fire to the school we had to use matches. Then get away as fast as we could," said the voice.

"Well, I've made something that means we don't have to be there when a fire starts."

"Say that again, Burner," said someone.

"Rob Turner," Jack said to himself.

"I'll show you," said Rob.

He took some things out of his bag and put them on the coffee table.

"This is a timer. This makes a spark. This is a small dish and this is a bottle of petrol. You join these two wires. You join this to the timer. You put the dish of petrol close to where the spark will be. Then you set the timer and walk away. The timer goes off. And whoosh! And we are far away watching the fun," he said.

"Does it work?" asked someone.

"I'll show you, Max," said Rob.

"That's Max Brown," Jack said to himself.

"Is it safe in here?" asked Max.

"It's safe," said Rob.

But it wasn't. Rob had been drinking in the pub. Now he was drinking vodka.

He put too much petrol into the dish. "Look for the spark," he said.

But what he got was a loud bang and a dish full of flames. The Blazer Boys jumped back and over went the coffee table. The dish of flames went flying.

Blazing petrol splashed onto the carpet, a chair and Max Brown.

Chapter 10

All three started to burn. Max began running and screaming as panic swept through the room faster than fire.

The torch went out as it was kicked over in the rush.

Now the only light in the room was coming from the flames.

They were growing and spreading fast.

Max tore off his burning jacket and threw it to the floor. The rest of The Blazers were yelling and crashing into each other as they tried to find the window. It was every man for himself. Suddenly, fire was no longer fun.

Upstairs, Jack turned on his torch.

"What are we waiting for?" he asked.

But Mike couldn't hear him. He was holding his head and rocking from side to side. The loud bang, the flames and the screaming had sent his mind back into the past.

"Landmine! Get back. Get back," was all he could say.

"Oh, no. Not now. Come on, Mike. We've got to get out. We could die in here!" said Jack.

Downstairs, The Blazer Boys had opened the window. But as they went rushing out, air came rushing in.

The air began feeding the flames. An armchair was on fire and thick, black smoke began filling the room.

More flames went racing up the curtains. The fire was spreading at a frightening speed. There were flames everywhere.

Jack wanted to run but he stayed with Mike. He dragged him onto the landing.

"Come on, Mike. We've got to get going. We've got to get out!" he shouted.

But how were they going to get out? Flames were waiting in the room below. Thick, black smoke was creeping up the stairs.

It was getting into Jack's eyes, nose and lungs.

It was choking the life out of him. Just when it seemed that fire would take two lives, Mike's mind cleared.

He looked around and said, "Bloody hell, Jack. Time to get out of here."

Putting his jacket around Jack's head, he picked him up and ran downstairs through the fire.

The flames licked around them and Jack felt as if his whole body was about to catch fire.

Mike kept going until they were outside. Jack's clothes had begun to burn and Mike beat out the flames with his bare hands.

Their clothes and hair were smoking. But they were alive.

It was then that Mike saw Max Brown lying on the ground. He was bleeding badly from a cut across his neck.

The rest of the Blazer Boys were nowhere to be seen.

Mike said, "He's cut himself on the broken window. It's bad. He'll bleed to death if we don't get him some help. I'll try to stop the bleeding but you've got to run for help. You need to be quick."

He went on, "Go down the driveway of the big house and turn right onto the lane. It's a mile from there to the main road. Find a phone or stop a car. Now go."

Jack set off. But it hurt every time he breathed in and his legs felt like jelly.

The mile to the main road felt more like ten. His lungs were on fire, and he was feeling faint by the time he got there.

When a car came along, he stepped into the road and waved his arms.

"Stop! I need help!" he shouted.

But the car swerved past him and didn't stop. Two more cars did the same thing.

"_____," Jack shouted at them.

The next car slowed to a stop and Jack gasped out, "Fire at New Hall. Someone is bleeding to death. Please help us." Then he fell to the ground.

The next thing he knew he was being wheeled into a room in the hospital.

A nurse looked at his legs and said,
"I'll have to cut your trousers off you.
Your burns need treating."

"You can't cut my trousers off," said Jack.

"Why not?" asked the nurse.

"I haven't got any underpants on,"
said Jack.

"Well, why not?" asked the nurse.

"I left them in a police station," said Jack.

The nurse gave him a puzzled look.
Then she gave him a towel and started
cutting his trousers.

"I was in a fire," said Jack.

The nurse smiled. "I can see that,"
she said.

"Do you know what happened to Mike
and Max Brown?" asked Jack.

"Who?" asked the nurse.

"They were in the fire as well," said Jack.

"You're the only one who's come in so
far," said the nurse.

But just as she spoke, the doors of the room opened and Mike came in on a trolley. Jack's burns were painful, but they didn't stop a smile spreading all over his face.

Mike said, "Good running, Jack. They got Max Brown to hospital just in time. And thanks for staying with me back there in the cottage. I'd shake your hand but that will have to wait."

For the first time, Jack saw how badly Mike had been burnt.

Mike went on, "I'd call that a good night's work. The Blazer Boys are finished and we've got the proof we need to clear your name."

"Thanks to you," said Jack.

"Thanks to J.A.M.," said Mike.

The nurse still looked puzzled. "Come on. It's bed for you," she said.

She wheeled Jack out of the room.

"See you tomorrow!" shouted Mike.

"You bet you will!" Jack shouted back.

Jack was put to bed and given something to ease the pain. As he went to sleep he knew that life was going to get better.

What he didn't know was that on his first day back at school, everyone would stand up and clap as he was given a medal for his bravery.

He didn't know his running would get so good that he'd run *for* the school. Not *away* from it. And he didn't know that he would ask Anna out and she'd say "yes".

As Mike kept telling him, "You never know what you can do until you try."

Look out for other exciting stories in the
Survival series:

About the author

Have you ever been hunted by the police, chased by a gang, or tried to stay alive after a plane crash?

If you have, then you know the name of the game is survival. If you haven't, why not read about the teenagers in my stories. They find getting into trouble is easy. It's the getting out of trouble that's the hard bit.

I spent three years training to be a teacher and 33 years being one. I always wanted to know how hard it would be to write books for teenagers. Now I know!

Pete Guppy

SURVIVAL

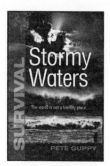

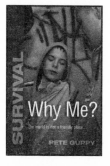

in association with

NASEN House, 4/5 Amber Business Village, Amber Close, Amington,
Tamworth, Staffordshire B77 4RP

·

Rising Stars UK Ltd.
22 Grafton Street, London W1S 4EX
www.risingstars-uk.com

Text © Rising Stars UK Ltd.

The right of Pete Guppy to be identified as the author of this work has
been asserted by him in accordance with the Copyright, Design and
Patents Act, 1988.

Published 2009

Cover design: Roger Warham
Cover image: Horizon International Images Limited/Alamy
Text design and typesetting: Roger Warham
Publisher: Gill Budgell
Editorial consultant: Lorraine Petersen

British Library Cataloguing in Publication Data.

A CIP record for this book is available from the British Library.

ISBN: 978-1-84680-600-1

Printed in the UK by CPI Bookmarque, Croydon, CR0 4TD

Mixed Sources
Product group from well-managed
forests and other controlled sources
www.fsc.org Cert no. TT-COC-002227
© 1996 Forest Stewardship Council